Copyright © 2023 James Rudi

The moral right of the author has been asserted. Apart from any fair dealing for the purposes of research or private study, or criticism or review, as permitted under the Copyright, Designs and Patents Act 1988, this publication may only be reproduced, stored or transmitted, in any form or by any means, with the prior permission in writing of the publishers, or in the case of reprographic reproduction in accordance with the terms of licences issued by the Copyright Licensing Agency. Enquiries concerning reproduction outside those terms should be sent to the publishers.

This is a work of fiction. Names, characters, businesses, places, events and incidents are either the products of the author's imagination or used in a fictitious manner. Any resemblance to actual persons, living or dead, or actual events is purely coincidental.

Matador
Unit E2 Airfield Business Park
Harrison Road, Market Harborough
Leicestershire. LE16 7UL
Tel: 0116 2792299
Email: books@troubador.co.uk
Web: www.troubador.co.uk/matador
Twitter: @matadorbooks

ISBN 978 180514 3499

British Library Cataloguing in Publication Data.
A catalogue record for this book is available from the British Library.

Matador is an imprint of Troubador Publishing Ltd

HARAMBE
Tales of a Wonderer

by James Rudi

Part 1: Diary of a Pleasure Seeker

The Apartment	5	The Church	22
The Café	9	The Bar	26
The Hotel	13	The City	29
The Park	17	The Party	36

Part 2: Tales of a Wonderer

Papa	47	Herve	64
Pacho I	48	Pacho II	65
Clark	49	Harambe I	67
Gabrielle	51	Sandra	69
Moondog	53	Royale	70
Margot	54	White Feather	71
Herve and Pacho	55	Jon the Baptist	72
Harry	57	The Doctor	73
The Market Trader	60	Mia	74
The Lawyer	61	Harry, Clark and	
The Dealer	62	Moondog	75
Cleo	63	Harambe II	76

Part 3: Notes from a Collection

News Article	79	Harry's Story	83
Collected People	80	Margot's Poem	84
Acquired Things	81	Pacho's Ballad	85
Discovered Words	82		

PART 1
Diary of a Pleasure Seeker

THE APARTMENT

I wake early with the first light coming through the net curtains and wonder whom I may have offended or delighted the day before and whether I might try again today.

I sit up and finish the dregs of yesterday's coffee and the end of a cigarette in the ashtray, then go back to sleep until I am woken properly an hour later by the sounds of street life trickling through the open window.

Turning on the radio, the bass hits my delicate stomach, and I switch the station to listen to a symphony that transports me to a half-sleep-dream-state with my eyes closed and a soft smile on my face, considering the possibilities of the day ahead.

As the music finishes, I take that to signal the start of my mischief and roll out of bed with a thud and a chuckle, knocking over a small pile of books which I still haven't delivered to the booksellers.

Above them, an empty wine glass sits on the side, and a half-empty bottle beside it, testament to the evening before.

I change the radio once again in search of something livelier, before realising the day and switching it off altogether, closing the window, and adding a little calm and silence. I take my place on a stool beneath the window and stare at nothing in particular until my head clears.

In the gardens below, an ancient oak is glistening in the sun and the pallet of greens provides a gentle focus for my attention as I stir myself to life. A few moments later, the day insists, and I am beckoned.

Ready and spruced for the occasion of a new day, I prepare to leave the apartment with my notepad, pencil and wallet, checking to see how much is left of each from yesterday's antics and what it will afford me this morning. All are in good supply and I head out, ready for breakfast.

Opening my door and stepping into the hallway, I have the misfortune to bump into a neighbour I don't know or like particularly well. We exchange niceties while he collects his morning newspaper with daily updates on the fame and misfortunes of the rich and deviant. It will no doubt give him all the tuts and grumbles he needs to get him through his day.

In the ground floor lobby, a man is hunched over cleaning the carpets, and looks up at me with a grunt and a blank look, not so much as a furrowed brow, before continuing his silent work.

Suddenly remembering something I have forgotten, I return home, only to bump into my neighbour once again on my way back out, who mutters some otherism.

I like brevity and he challenges the fine art, droning on about nothing in detail. Perhaps he has never had the pleasure of silence, so he fills the void to escape falling into this own thoughts. I drown it out with my own inner voice, before I look at my watch, lie and excuse myself with places to be and time ticking on. I am nothing but politeness and patience with this man, who is simply going about his own mundane business.

I tell myself if a third encounter should follow today, I would like to shake him by the shoulders and demand something interesting, or nothing ever again, then I do my best to avoid him for the rest of the day.

With a swing in my step and the scent of cut grass in the air, I stroll off the apartment steps into the morning sunshine, towards the cafes and hotels opposite the park, through streets where people and vehicles mingle with the birds in their routines, the morning cacophony rising and falling like music.

In search of a lazy day and with a cool breeze on my cheek, I remember once again my rush nowhere and slow myself to an amble with a deep breath, surrendering to the day's pace. In that instant, I am pulled sharply into the present and everything is illuminated with greater clarity, as if I had not been looking properly before. A passing woman holding a child appears as if peeled from a cinema screen. A round window high on a huge wall comes into focus and I wonder how I hadn't seen that before. And then as quickly as the moment came, thought got involved and the sensation evaporated, returning me to the faint ordinariness of the day.

THE CAFÉ

In a busy café situated on the corner of a salacious-looking hotel, with crushed velvet curtains and harlequin murals, I order my food at the counter and take a seat, facing the window and the world outside.
A man is typing furiously on his machine next to me and I lean over with a disarming smile and ask him what is so important. He has an important job, he sighs, with responsibilities and deadlines and needs a well-earned holiday. Monkey say monkey do I think to myself. I tell him I am sorry to hear that, maybe he should have a life that he doesn't need a holiday from. He looks confused, like a child unable to make sense of new information, lost for a moment, before turning to me to distract from the apparent truth.
He is wearing the customary clown uniform of the modern successful man, a crisp shirt, pressed trousers, good hair, shoes and watch, but somehow, they make him look ridiculous, for everything shows him naked. I think to myself that I could

never take myself that seriously, for that would be a mockery of the game I prefer to play, which I take very seriously.

He has an air of silent superiority, as if his virtues are entwined with his visible success. The way he looks at me suggests he isn't used to talking to lesser people and that we could have nothing in common other than mutual contempt.

The man asks me what I do for a living. I reply saying that's a dull question, ask me something else or tell me something amazing. He pauses for a minute, struck by the challenge, then declares that he once collected beer cans and sent one to the edge of space on a balloon. I tell him that is a much better effort, do more of that.

My breakfast arrives and I do my best to enjoy each mouthful, but too much stimulus and inspiration surrounds me, so I reach for my notebook and scrawl to see what comes out, whilst shovelling the food almost oblivious to taste and texture.

Intrusive thoughts and ideas are welcomed, which a friend has informed and diligently warned me borders on dysfunction, just short of schizophrenia. I have some choice in what I let out, or in, apparently, but it's fun playing with that line to see what happens.

In the kitchen, a plate smashes, breaking through the white noise and I enjoy the echo and the raised voices that follow.

Surveying the room, I find myself observing two ladies seated at a table by the counter, one eating, the other talking in a ceaseless stream at the friend, twiddling her knife and fork as she speaks and gestures. When her quiet friend does eventually speak, alpha female puts her hands behind her head and leans out, dominating her opponent with her body instead of her mouth, before interrupting and taking over the conversation once again.

After twenty minutes watching this charade whilst eating, drawing and writing in my notebook, I pay the bill and wander over to alpha.

Smiling warmly and excusing myself for the interruption as politely as I can, I tell her I've been watching them awhile, and that maybe she could leave some air in the conversation for her friend to speak.

She looks stunned, as if she has been slapped, babbling something in a desperate defence while her friend smirks and shrinks.

I say nothing more, tip my head to them both, and

walk off while the balance of power behind me shifts for a moment, or alpha's self-image implodes. I don't mind either way.

THE HOTEL

I wander next door into the hotel and pass by the front desk, wishing good morning to the receptionist, who doesn't look pleased or look up.
Finding myself a comfortable but worn leather armchair in the corner of the lobby, I flick through the morning papers for a flavour of the moment, of what people are reading and thinking. The only story that calls out from amongst the ever-repetitive sagas of society, life and death, is a small article about a pensioner caught in a field by police with his manhood in a horse's mouth. I appreciate the audacity and let my grin become a hearty chuckle, before copying it into my notebook to type up later.
On a bookshelf more ornamental than library, a pile of books catches my interest and I peruse a few, discovering cursory facts and stories to add to my mental and written collections.
Wondering what I wish to do next, I stroll to the bar overlooking the park and take a seat on a high stool with my arms crossed and chin rested. There is a

whirring fan on the counter, and for no good reason I stick my finger in its cover, catching the end on the blades harder than I anticipated.

Pulling my arm back fast, I knock and break a vase and it cuts my hand before it falls. It's not deep, but the napkins which I grab from the counter turn red quickly enough and pressure takes a while to stem the bleeding. Flowers and glass cover the floor around me and it looks both enchanting and tragic.

The receptionist emerges and wants to know what happened, and why I am in the bar. Looking at the mess, she checks that I am okay with mild but genuine sympathy, then asks me to leave, showing me the exit to the side street. She tells me there is a chemist nearby, rather than the hospital two miles away. I oblige and thank her for her impeccable goodness and hand her a handsome tip.

As I step into the alley beside the hotel, glancing around to gauge my bearings, I see a bicycle strewn between some bins, with no lock or apparent owner. It meets my needs perfectly, I have a long day ahead and tell myself I will return it later, perhaps.

It is then that I notice further down the alley, a man laying face down. His hands are bloodied, as if he has just fallen from the roof, and I look up four flights of fire stairs and assume he is dead, wondering what civilised world finds a man like this perished alone in an alley. Then I see his back rise and fall and realise that he is very much alive.

Tentatively stepping closer, afraid of what I may be about to find, I lean over to see a pale and sickly-looking young face, and ask if he is alright. The young man suddenly sits bolt upright, as if nothing out of his ordinary, slurring some explanation about climbing out of the window, pointing to the second floor. I cannot tell whether it is true or if he just confused.

I ask him whether he needs some help and he says he'll be fine, before standing, then climbing on to the bike and disappearing as if nothing had happened.

Somewhat bemused and relieved, I shake my head and go in the direction of the chemists.

When I arrive, there is a patient already in the consulting room, so I wait, perusing the shelves of hocus medicines and tonics for life, until I am called by a nurse who tells me the chemist is busy for now but she will see me.

Raising my hand, I tell the nurse what happened

and she inspects my napkin-bandaged arm. She smiles playfully and when I half-laugh back, her mischief rises up and her smile becomes a wide-eyed look of possibility.

She is ordinary looking, but pretty when she doesn't mean to be. She looks again at my arm, tuts and shrugs, then talks to me while she cleans and dresses my wound.

As she is finishing, I think about seducing her, and the twinkle in her eyes and playful touching of her hair gives me the notion she is thinking the same. But the bell goes as another customer comes into the store, so she finishes up and I wait outside to pay, then leave, sounding the bell behind me.

THE PARK

Late morning back in the spring sunshine, I head into the park, where children are buzzing about, picnics are being laid out and flies swatted away. Ducks and geese jostle for position.
It reminds me for the briefest moment of an occasion and a feeling from a long time ago, and I push it to the back of my mind and follow the path of least bustle.
It is then that I remember the small bag of dried mushrooms in my pocket, and the nonsense neighbour encounter when I had gone back to retrieve them. They should provide for a nice mellow tint to the afternoon, but I misjudge their potency and the next hour becomes a waving and pulsating ride, as I wander carefully, catching snippets of conversation that only add to the confusion, holding myself together just long-enough to find a bench to contain myself. This is short-lived and the descent takes hold.
A man sat on an opposite bench is holding his dog whilst they both take a rest. His face begins

to melt and his dog morphs and becomes a wolf, and I have to look away.

Further in the distance, a group of elderly women and men are exercising and their motions blur and I cannot take much more.

Excusing myself to nobody, I go to lay on the grass and close my eyes When I open them again, the clouds are breathing. I lay there for what seems like an eternity, mesmerised, until the sensation settles down and I can sit up.

Everything now has a bright glow and a subtle twinkle, and wherever I look closely, there is a depth beyond comprehension, from the wrinkles in my clothes to the grain and terrain of my skin.

The grass appears as an orchestra, violin strings waving in the wind in symphonic harmony. I imagine it playing and wonder if maybe it does.

Then as if divinely created for this moment, drifting in from beneath a nearby tree, I hear a musician playing Spanish guitar. It is delicate and beautiful on the soul and I listen enchanted, realising he is playing for no one but himself. I accept my concert for one and let it wash over me with the breeze. My whole body and mind relax and my fingers and hands play along in the air to their own dance.

Above me, three squabbling crows suddenly scream and dive and I am stirred from my reverie as they pass between me and the music, jostling with one another mid-air before flying into the distance.

Returning to my sense of self, and looking around for nothing in particular, my eye is drawn to a pink toy in the grass. With typical curiosity, I lean over and pick it up, spinning its wheels which still work, though the body is mostly cracked and broken. I am taken by the dull texture and appearance, set against the soft features of the grass and flowers, and wonder where old toys go to die. I decide I should give it a proper burial and set myself the task.

At the side of some flower beds where the soil is loose, I dig a small hole with a found stick and lay the toy to rest at the edge. I pass up the typical ceremony and conduct my own, asking the grass if they knew him well and if anyone had any final words, before lowering the discarded and once-loved toy into its eternal home. A makeshift posy from the flower-beds completes the grave and I take a daisy for my jacket button-hole to continue my walk.

Strolling towards the city end of the park, clouds begin to pepper the sky and shadows from the trees fade the colours and hues of the grass into one. I can smell rain coming.

I talk to dogs that come to sniff me out, avoiding their owners whenever possible, who only ever apologise for their dogs bothering me. I never mind the dogs, only the owners' attempts to apologise for something they cannot or will not control.

One dog stays for a while as its owner strolls in from the distance, and I tell it about my morning and the man in the alley. When the owner arrives I ask the dog's name, Louis the Elephant, she says. I reply this is the second-best dog name I've heard and she asks me the first, but I won't tell her and she looks annoyed.

Walking on, I settle on a shady spot near the water pools and take a moment to look around. Amongst the panorama of park life, I see a barefoot man dressed in short-sleeve shirt and shorts walk straight through the water fountains and I like his stride, not breaking a beat. Suddenly, he walks towards me and a pile of bags not three feet from where I am sat, and I find myself next to him on the grass while he dries off in the warm afternoon air.

As he sits, I introduce myself and ask if the water was cold. The man says yes, but that he doesn't mind, he is cleaner and cooler. It is then that I realise he is homeless, at least for now, though he seems quite at home here in the park.

I inquire what brings him here and he explains how he lost his home in the grounds of a school where he worked as caretaker for many years. Retirement wasn't meant to look like this, but such is life. He tells me how he finds it on the streets and the kindness and ambivalence of passersby, how he has his routines and manages better than many. He says we are all ordinary people and any one of us could be here. He is stoic and good humoured and I do not patronise him with pity.

I comment on his colourful tobacco pouch and he offers it to me as a gift, asking for a few coins in return if I have them. I offer him a smoke and we sit together, rolling and smoking.

We talk quietly for a while longer about other things, then I excuse myself, giving him enough money for a meal and a bed, then head east.

THE CHURCH

Mid-afternoon is pressing on and as I leave the park revitalised, and walk into the city, skies have turned grey. Moments later clouds open and unleash torrential rain.
While others dash for cover, I step into it and stay there, happily drenched, wiping water over my face and through my hair, until deciding to shelter somewhere warm and dry to sit and think.
As car rooves and umbrellas spatter, I make my way into a church, turning on the top steps beneath its vast portico, just as it slows and the sky clears behind me. Standing for a moment, wet but sunny skies leave a rainbow and I think how fitting, as I walk beneath the arched doors into the bowels of god's house.
Entering the crypt, I hear angels singing and light speaking. The mushrooms are wearing off, but they leave their imprint on my soul.
A beggar is asking around for any change and I give him what I have left loose in my pocket, expecting and receiving no thanks.

Looking up at the stained-glass windows high above the columns, they cast a kaleidoscope of light of every colour. Below them, I light a candle and say no prayer, but thank my own god, standing for a few moments of perfect peace and appreciation. The near silence is impeccable.

Walking back out through the doors, admiring the blind faith of men to follow men, I wonder if women leading women would be any different.

Outside, people occupy benches all around the garden courtyard, and I find one empty to bask alone and watch the world go by.

As I sit back and make myself comfortable, I hear 'Excuse me young man' from an elder stateswoman looking and walking in my direction. She is well dressed and genteel, of many yesteryears gone by.

I am charmed and reply 'yes young lady', and she smiles back with her whole face. She asks if she can join me, as we're both alone, I say of course, room enough for two.

She asks after my day, to which I reply it is still going but we'll see at the end.

We chit chat a little and she comments on the flower in my button-hole, then I search for more. I ask what brings her to this moment and place.

She tells me she is the granddaughter of the founder of a theatre around the corner, and there to see her grandson perform this evening. It is a very special night for her, she says. A long time ago, she adds, she was a mathematician for the government, doing complex work on probability, and we talk for a while about chance. She says formulas are the recording of god speaking and she comes to church to listen closer. I tell her that my father was the only one of five children to survive birth, so the likelihood of my existence is infinitesimally small. She agrees.

Then she asks what brings me here and I tell her a long path well-trodden. I say I have been many things to many people, such that on occasion I barely know myself. The things I've seen I can't recount, the things I've felt I can't escape, but these days I am just myself and my time, nothing to nobody, a simple pleasure seeker.

I share with her a story about my past, of when I was both father and child. When I have finished she looks amazed but unsurprised, then offers her empathy with her wise eyes. She replies that some people are made of glass, some of rubber, and some of oak, that when life occurs we can shatter, bounce or grow stronger. I understand and know.

I thank her for her wisdom, then ask her what other advice for life she might offer a stranger after these many generous years. She doesn't think long before declaring 'do what pleases you'. I say that is perfect and that maybe I could give her something in return. She says she would like that.

I tell her thar our existence is tiny compared to some living beings, that whales can live for two hundred years and some trees for millennia, fungi for more, every single one a trillion to one chance, briefly appearing for its moment in the sun. She doesn't say anything but nods her head in gentle understanding.

Before I leave, she asks me my name and I tell her Rufus, even though it isn't. I add, gesturing to the cavernous church behind us, to always listen to the rhythm, not the noise.

Then I put my hands together and bow my head at my new friend, and she does the same, and that is our farewell to our time together, parting in kind smiles and silence.

THE BAR

As late afternoon is turning into early evening, I head for the club to set things in motion, but it is too quiet and empty, so I take the steps down to the basement bar where virtues and lights are low and expectations and energy high.

A heady mix of people compete with the music, something samba-or-other, I cannot be sure. I order some olives, a glass of red wine and a rum chaser, then with my back to the bar, sipping away, I watch the room of vagrants and players starting to fill, a parade of the weird and wonderful.

One beautiful specimen walks past, with tailored yellow jacket and hand tattoos of scribbles and symbols recorded in skin and ink, striding confidently off to spar with fellow devils and deviants.

At the end of a long table, two men and a dog are playing chess at great speed. I take a seat on the long bench and watch. The man smoking his pipe asks if I know how to play, then introduces his playmate who doesn't look up, and his dog Rufus, to which I laugh and admire the chance of it, or not. I nod to the dog.

When the game ends, the man asks if I would like to hear a poem about chess. I accept and he begins a saga of the king who sacrificed everyone for his queen, until he saw that as his pawns turned, as are the rules of the game, they became royal, whereupon he bowed his head and apologised. It is an intelligent metaphor for humility, and I shake his hand in praise.

My glasses now empty, and thinking about another, I peruse the cocktail board on the wall and consider a rum-and-other concoction named after a famous gangster film, when a young miscreant seated opposite strikes up an unexpected and welcome conversation.

Chatting furiously and gesticulating joyfully, she shares her dystopian vision of the machine-made future, explaining her theory in fine detail. When she is done, I ask what she thinks will happen after all of this has come to pass. She says it's a great question, to which I agree. She thinks for a moment, then speculates that humans will become a zoo attraction for the robots, and they shall take our identities, and we both laugh.

I like this, it isn't the typical small talk, defying the nonsense and politics and endless analysis of daily life. This is imagination meeting the absurd on the way to the sublime.

I tell her she reminds me of a woman I knew once a long time ago, she has the same spirit of life in her. Before I have to leave, I offer her a drink and we share a tequila and a kiss together.

I head for the stairs, slowing to see the many framed pictures posted on the walls and ceiling, of past performers, players and staff. One has a trio of hatted and suited musicians with their instruments, and I wonder when they passed these stairs.

I reach the top and step into the rhythm of the street outside.

THE CITY

The evening air is cooling, and I light a cigarette for the stroll. As I pass between a gap in the buildings, the setting sunlight hits my cheek and I stop and turn to face it, closing my eyes for a moment and enjoying the warmth, until a car horn shatters the air and brings me back into the here and now.

Watching the many faces and bodies and motions of city life, beautiful hijab eyes approach and I flirt with them as they pass, the hidden beauty more sensuous than the readily seen.

A grocer is animatedly selling the last bowls of produce and buckets of bunched and wilting flowers, loudly discoursing with a colleague about a large green elephant somewhere nearby, disparaging it as art.

In the borders of the business district, near to where it meets the theatres and taverns, I bump into an old associate drowning his sorrows in the entrance to an inn. He looks surprised but pleased to see me, it has been a long time, and he shares his food enthusiastically, asking the waitress for a second plate. While we eat, we exchange small talk and offer reflection on our recent lives. He is a fine raconteur and makes for good listening.

Clients are thin on the ground he says, he doesn't think the year will play out well. I tell him worry is interest on a debt he may never owe. He thanks me and offers to buy me a drink.

He then tells me about a client he met earlier that day, accused of an assault on someone for being different, adding that people are closed-minded on the biggest and smallest of things. I agree with him and he seems a little less burdened, what is normal anyway, I add.

With conversation thinning and awkward silence approaching, we finish our drinks and part ways with a handshake and insincere promises to get together again soon.

Back on the street, I walk purposefully towards the river. The sun is taking its final bow below scattered clouds, reflecting oranges and pinks in the windows of towering merchant buildings on both banks and stretching into the horizon.

Evening is now pushing through to night, beckoning the mischief makers and urchins, the best and worst of people. Possibility is in the air.

plate. While we eat, we exchange small talk and offer reflection on our recent lives. He is a fine raconteur and makes for good listening.

Clients are thin on the ground he says, he doesn't think the year will play out well. I tell him worry is interest on a debt he may never owe. He thanks me and offers to buy me a drink.

He then tells me about a client he met earlier that day, accused of an assault on someone for being different, adding that people are closed-minded on the biggest and smallest of things. I agree with him and he seems a little less burdened, what is normal anyway, I add.

With conversation thinning and awkward silence approaching, we finish our drinks and part ways with a handshake and insincere promises to get together again soon.

Back on the street, I walk purposefully towards the river. The sun is taking its final bow below scattered clouds, reflecting oranges and pinks in the windows of towering merchant buildings on both banks and stretching into the horizon.

Evening is now pushing through to night, beckoning the mischief makers and urchins, the best and worst of people. Possibility is in the air.

THE CITY

The evening air is cooling, and I light a cigarette for the stroll. As I pass between a gap in the buildings, the setting sunlight hits my cheek and I stop and turn to face it, closing my eyes for a moment and enjoying the warmth, until a car horn shatters the air and brings me back into the here and now.

Watching the many faces and bodies and motions of city life, beautiful hijab eyes approach and I flirt with them as they pass, the hidden beauty more sensuous than the readily seen.

A grocer is animatedly selling the last bowls of produce and buckets of bunched and wilting flowers, loudly discoursing with a colleague about a large green elephant somewhere nearby, disparaging it as art.

In the borders of the business district, near to where it meets the theatres and taverns, I bump into an old associate drowning his sorrows in the entrance to an inn. He looks surprised but pleased to see me, it has been a long time, and he shares his food enthusiastically, asking the waitress for a second

Crossing the bridge above the boats and the moorings, I stop to take in the scene, from the centuries-old architecture in the fading light to the dark chopping waters below. I stand with my hands resting on the balustrade and contemplate jumping.

As I watch nothing and everything, I consider the many who may have gone before me and what brought them to conclude their ride early, judging none for their final decision. I think of my own shames and failings which I have grown to live with alongside my sorrows and joys.

I imagine too the myriad of lives and reasons that flow daily through cities, the billions of heartbeats and fleeting moments in every corner. From refugees to fortune seekers, lives fought and forged, and cities like it everywhere, each their own, but also the same.

I've stood here with the same thoughts many times before, recounting the value of my life and my time spent, each occasion re-affirming my deepest desire to live and breathe for even an hour more. I take a deep breath and continue on my way.

Upon reaching the other side, I see from above a courtyard beneath the bridge, which I think I know by reputation of the strange and unusual, but have never visited, and so I head down.

I find a spirit merchant open and step inside to buy a special bottle of rum I've heard about. An array of golden brown and green bottles look out from shelves running floor to ceiling, the most illustrious and rare behind locked glass cabinet doors.

Offering his assistance, I am met by a small obnoxious store owner, who delights in correcting my mispronunciation of the bottle I request. The unsmiling man behind the counter explains that's not how you say it, but I reply that is exactly how a man of my reputation should. I shall remember in future to pronounce it as the man has just taught me.

On the way out, I allow my hand to catch a display of cigar boxes, knocking them down, before smiling and apologising disingenuously over my shoulder. I pull the door quickly behind me and disappear into the night.

Turning the corner, and as if by some instant karmic order, my evening takes a sudden jolt as I am confronted by a picture of anger. A suited red-faced man is bellowing at a woman in the middle of a quiet street, a few inches from her cheek, and she is cowering.

Stopping in my tracks, I call out to ask if she is okay, but the man growls for me to mind my own business. When I say that I cannot, the man asks what I am going to do. I reply that I don't know and that's why the man must calm down.

I live for moments like this, that instant where everything can fall left or right. It is now or never. Flip a coin, win or lose, play to play, the tension begging to see what happens next.

It has been a very long time, I am not a man of violence, but I can keep this man at bay with my measured words and air of contained menace.

The little man full of hate and bravado doesn't like this, but I can see in his eyes that his power isn't real and he knows it, pausing for the briefest second before he finds out what neither of us knows yet.

Then he notices me shaking and calls me a coward. I tell him it is because I am afraid of myself, that he must leave now because I do not know what will happen next. His face changes to silent defeat and resignation, he walks away and it is over.

The woman wipes her face and marches off in another direction, emotionally bruised but thankfully not beaten.

I take a very deep breath and recover my equilibrium, the adrenaline subsiding with every breath, giving way to a terrific sense of euphoria.

Gathering myself once more, I take sanctuary in the windows of a parade of shops set back from the street, some open, most closed.

A gallery is open a few doors down, though the sign says closed. The lights are on and the door open, as workmen carry out tools and rubbish.

With a spirit of mischief, I put my head inside to look around for someone or no one, finding only a few large canvasses on the walls and a plethora of books lining shelves across the back.

I wander in and look around, until a young woman emerges and asks if she can help. I say no, and that I was just passing. She tells me to feel free to look around a few moments longer but then she is due to lock up and leave.

I admire the artworks and the craftmanship, though they are not to my taste, before seeing the stratospheric price tags, wondering at the audacity of the gallery, the artist and the buyer, all complicit in this little game of luxury and prestige.

As she returns to close and escort me out, I ask to know her favourite piece. She is flattered that someone should seek her private opinion and points to a small piece on the floor waiting to be hung, telling me briefly about its creator.

She then says that she is just finishing up after a show, and off to a party nearby where she doesn't really know anybody, would I consider joining her. I graciously accept and we small talk as we stroll into the night.

THE PARTY

We arrive at a townhouse in a fashionable part of town, where pristine facades hide the debauched and tumultuous insides.

My escort was not invited, but walks her way in with another guest none-the-wiser, seeing someone she knows as we enter. I lose her quickly as she pushes through the throng with gusto, leaving me alone with mischief in mind.

In the first of three large rooms, a lounge with high ceilings and many guests in various guises and conversations, a wide-eyed and sweaty man in the middle is juggling, while music is pounding and powders are strewn on mirrors. I find one table with several indeterminable chemical concoctions laid out. I don't know what it is, but partake in some anyway while nobody is paying attention.

Two women are patting themselves down, looking for something they've lost. They spot me and ask me to help them, before falling prey to their own intoxication and moving on in a torrent of conversation, forgetting I am there.

Though I have imbibed and enjoyed many sensory pleasures, more times than I can recall, I am always left with the feeling that they pale in comparison to real life. The freedom ascribed is boring and short-lived, a brief respite from dull lives, leaving most more hollow, with no new insight or experience.

Finding my stride, I pick up someone else's drink while they are not looking, repeating the trick twice more until I am caught red-handed and offer false apologies for picking up the wrong glass mistakenly, no suspicion or upset caused.

A woman curled up in a large armchair is playing a handmade wooden flute, along with the music from the speakers, and I let it wash over me. She sees me and smiles back, before I wander into the next room.

By no means intentionally, I find myself drawn into a conversation, where a young couple are banging their drum about progress and justice and this that and the other social issue, passionate in their many convictions.

I don't have time for this any longer, time is not on my side and I know what is important and not.

I listen quietly then ask them casually if they think they might be the problem.

Their faces change simultaneously, from intent certainty to a look of stunned confusion, the precursor to what will become outright outrage to my intellectual challenge and rude awakening.

With their faces frozen in disbelief, I press on and say voting and violence haven't worked for a thousand years, maybe they don't. If they really wanted to be defiant, they could try apathy, turn their backs on everything they complain about, don't fight it, ignore it. Is there not a more honest way to exist than to do so on one's own terms, not as a response, but as life itself. Does not everything else seem futile.

I ask them too if maybe they don't need to change the world. I suggest they could make their own game, lay their own train track and generally not give a single care.

They look confused, which I recognise, but it doesn't matter, I can ask questions that don't need answering.

Then they decide they don't like me at all and the mood shifts to agitation. She says I need a reality check. I reply that reality is not my area of expertise anymore, but I'll try for her sake.

With a genuine inquisitiveness, I ask if they are not

just happy to be alive, is it not enough to make it to the end of the day? The man replies that he thinks that's a pretty low bar for living. I suggest that it is perhaps the highest bar indeed, that I have my limbs, my mind, a little money in my pocket and clothes on my back. They relax a little, leaning into the conversation and I can see them tentatively recalibrating their perspective. I seize their interest and present another lens to look through.

I suggest the way they think started before they could walk and talk, the lessons and labels they've collected, their morality, empathy, behaviour, none of us can help but absorb and become our surroundings, particularly in a world filled with leaders and the easily led.

But, if we quieten the noise and let things be, those things that don't matter have a way of dissipating, then all you are left with is what does. But what does anything matter anyway, I conclude.

Then I thank them for their company and leave, wobbling a little as I stand and head for the balcony and air.

On the busy terrace, I light a smoke, near to where a group are chatting, taking a few seconds to myself to absorb the day and its meanderings before zoning out.

Nearby, a chemically-inspired Christian is espousing the history of the bible. I listen and laugh quietly to myself as he streams theory and theology to his audience at a frenzied pace, making sure I don't get drawn in and drowned.

A lone and wandering young woman is collecting quotes, a beautiful inquisitive spirit looking for wisdom in all her youth and eagerness. She smells of warm and foreign shores, wearing bracelets and necklaces of equal charm and seductiveness as her scent. We speak for a short while and I offer her a gem for her collection, something I was told myself a long time ago: If you don't ask you don't get. It's not the best in my arsenal, but it seems apt and she likes it. Then I remember another and tell her 'do what pleases you', and this pleases her more.

I tell her that I collect interesting people and she is delighted to think that I consider her a classic addition. I show her my notebook and she is wide-eyed at the many things she finds. She thanks me for sharing, then slinks away into the rabble in search of her next slice of life.

Returning inside, I move into the far room, a dimly lit study where unfamiliar eastern music is playing. There is a distinctive and pungent scent of incense, which I cannot place in my mind's eye. I take a seat nowhere in particular, minding my own business and watching everyone else.

Floor cushions are scattered with books and bottles, and lamps give off a warm and gentle light, with candles casting shadows around the room. On a small table is a tall triangular prism, beside an even larger black stone obelisk as smooth as silk, and I stare at both for a while, imagining the stone as old as earth.

A shifty-looking man holding court with a shisha pipe in hand, calls out from across the room and asks if he knows me from somewhere, as the young woman I arrived with and her friend enter and take a place amongst the floor cushions where I join them. Unlikely I tell him, I am nothing to nobody.

The man frowns and says he is someone famous but I don't care. I tell him fame is its own slave and freedom its richer master. I ask if he remembers the last time he was a nobody. He finds this to his liking, no need for hot air or hubris tonight.

He is tanned and once-chiselled, showing signs of a hearty life in his paunch and his skin, an older better version of himself now. His sweeping black mane, with whisps of grey, and the air of a practised reprobate, shirt unbuttoned half-way, only adds to the character of himself he portrays.

Something about him tells me I've arrived in the right moment and I remember the rum in my pocket. I pour generously into two used glasses from one of the small coffee tables, passing him one, and we clink them together.

Next to him is an ornate pack of cards, with images of ancient nudes and goddesses on the back and gold foil around the edges. I ask if he plays and he says not very well, but we can try nonetheless. I suggest something simple, blackjack perhaps, and when I teasingly ask what we're playing for, he offers a gentleman's bet. I suggest we might play for something better. I offer him the chance to win my finger, but if he loses, I win a night with his wife, a tattered but beautiful and silent creature at his side. She is startled by the proposition, but not opposed. He grimaces in mixed-delight and looking at her for confirmation, agrees it a fair bet.

We play and he draws an impossible series of cards and I lose overwhelmingly. His skill is poor, but his luck outrageous, and I accept with grace. I immediately reach into my pocket and pull out my hand with middle finger outstretched, pointing it at his face, and he roars with laughter. Have my finger, I say. We shake hands and have another rum and he says I still owe him a finger.

Remembering my earlier conversation with Lady Chance, I ask him if he has heard of a micromort. He says no, so I tell him it is a unit representing a one in a million chance of death, that of the many different activities we do every day each has its own exacting measurement of risk and reward, much like cards.

He laughs again and passes the shisha pipe, telling me he shall call me Zarathustra, after a character in one of his favourite books, which I pretend not to know.

With my head starting to whir, I point out to nobody in particular that there is more beauty and perfection in the plumes of hookah smoke than all of man's work, and I watch as it swirls and twists in the invisible ether.

It is only then that I realise the scent is opium. As my body floats and space feels lighter, I hear voices muffle and watch as faces blur away. I close my eyes and fall into a deep slumber, dreaming of yet more faces that I cannot make out.

I wake in a daze to an empty room, as the owners are evicting the last guests and they ask if I am okay. They could not be kinder and I don't want to take liberties or become a liability. There is no sign of the woman I came with, so I oblige and head for the door. Looking down I see all fingers present.

Before I leave, I remember the article in my notebook and on the doorstep read it aloud to my hosts and a small group gathered at the door. When I finish, I break out laughing. Nobody else finds it funny, but it doesn't matter and that makes me enjoy it all the more, until tears stream down my face and the door closes behind me.

And now I am in the street, utterly lost. I stop once more to find myself, aware of this fresh moment, and I pause, putting my hands together and pointing upwards to the dark sky, in thanks for the end and beginning of another day, before I smile to nobody and go again.

PART 2
Tales of a Wonderer

PAPA

Harambe is another year older tomorrow. We shall go fishing early and catch our lunch, but he must sleep now and dream of heavenly things.

The next day when we fish, he sits at the end of the boat while I tell him stories, of people and places and adventures, until I can think of no more.

When I finish, I tell him he must make his own stories and have his own to tell. The world is all yours, I tell him, you can do anything, go anywhere, be anyone you want to be. Or you can be nothing and nobody too and that is okay as well, because it is all part of the story and there is no right or wrong, there is just the way it is.

I tell him that life is a bloom, a god-head, that it appears for him as a blank piece of paper to make of it his own, with simply the law of breath to keep, everything else is only as he writes it in the book of life, the journey he takes from nothing into nothing.

We row back to the shore and when we have pulled the boat onto the sand, we walk back to prepare our lunch and the rest of our stories.

PACHO I

We share a room and fight constantly. He tells me my mother is a whore and I tell him he is a son-of-a-bitch. We laugh and cry and care for nobody else. We speak of the crimes we would commit together and how we would get away with them. We talk of the people we would seduce and the adventures we would take them on. And we mean it, this is not talk, this is our will, our rules, our lives.

And then for reasons beyond my understanding we part ways for nearly a decade, I do not know whether he is dead or alive, in prison perhaps, or somewhere on the other side of the world with a family, or none. I think about Harambe often and it makes me smile just remembering. We were the finest of friends through the worst of times and that made us brothers for all our days.

CLARK

We met at a street market where he was bartering over a brass heron close to where I was stood, watching and waiting. He didn't buy it, or want it apparently, then bumped into me as he turned away, laughing and apologising at the same time, knocking my cigarette to the floor. Then he reached into his pocket and removed an old tobacco tin, offering to roll me another, and I accepted in good humour.

We shared a smoke beneath a tree at the edge of the market, sipping cheap coffee and talking about some of the many things and people we had seen there, speculating their stories.

He didn't tell me much about himself, though he said he was once in a cell with a psychopath and a sociopath and that he may well have been at least one of them.

I told him my friends Harry and Moondog would like him, and that we should all four go for drinks.

He called me Cluck, not because he couldn't pronounce my name, but because it was better suited to me he said. I called him Ram in return, as if it should fit him like a glove. And we were bonded forever. Before I left the market, I went back and stole the brass heron for my new friend.

GABRIELLE

I see him watching me on the terrace at Noah's Bar while he smokes and drinks coffee. He tells me later I move so gracefully and naturally, I make it look effortless. I explain it is the flow of motion meeting the rhythm of life, so I lean in and follow where it takes me.

He offers me a cigarette and we smoke together, watching the ducks and swans on the river. He says he has come there to look for yellow-tipped butterflies, but has not seen one yet today. A dragonfly lands on his shoulder but he doesn't see and before I can tell him it flies off again.

Later that evening, we dance together in the street to the music floating out from one of the bars. He asks me if I knew that the history of dance was as long as mankind, from celebrations to wars. Then we kiss goodnight.

The next day, around his neck I see a beautiful stone on a leather necklace, an opal sparkling with greens and blues and pinks, unpolished and natural, like a small universe.

He called me Gigi when we spoke on the phone, every month for more than twenty years, but we only ever met once again and I don't think he recognised me when I visited him. I kissed him and cried and that was the end of our story.

MOONDOG

Harambe was playing the piano the first time I saw him across a large empty room. I started humming away in recognition, when he turned around suddenly, with a beaming smile on his face and arms outstretched, welcoming and inviting me to sit beside him. He showed me the notes to strike alongside him and we played together in harmony.

I fell in love with Harambe. He and I were of the same spirit and we were drawn to each other immediately. Harry and Clark would love him equally, but it was different for me, it was a full mutual understanding from the very start, in recognition of each other's deeper nature.

One day sat on the beach, he tells me a story of how he and a friend used to pickpocket wealthy Arabs wearing their traditional garments. Often their long pockets held bundles of money, but one day they pulled out a bar of hashish, which they smoked and sold with equal pleasure.

He rolls a joint as he finishes the tale, his hands and arms tanned, grinning from the memory. We smoke it together and then swim and laugh in the glittering waves until the sun goes down.

MARGOT

We are on a train crossing America. It is morning and I notice him looking at the book I am reading as he notices me looking at the missing tip of his thumb.

He tells me he is getting off at Utah to meet a friend. I tell him my family are waiting for me in Chicago.

We speak for many hours as the landscape changes constantly through the windows. He isn't like most other people. He asks many questions about my journey and my plans, listening intently and looking deep into my face, though he never once looks at my scars, only my eyes, as if he sees all of me in there.

Before he leaves, I ask if I can take his photo. He declines politely, but suggests I could take another, maybe of his hands. I agree and he places them against the moving window, silhouetted by the low sun above the mountains.

After he has left, I sit for a long time staring out the window, before I close my eyes and say a little prayer in thanks.

HERVE AND PACHO

We lived together in an apartment above a restaurant where Harambe seemed to know everybody. He had introduced us as fellow reprobates and thought we should drink and fish together, which we did many times.

One day he tells us he has heard of a special place about an hour away and suggests we make the trip there the next morning before the sun rises. When we arrive and park the car, we ask him if he knows what he is looking for. He says we will know it when we see it.

And then the lake emerged over a bank and we had arrived, a tranquil sanctuary of nature, sky and peace. The surface of the water was completely still, save for a rowing boat tied to a tree, bobbing in the breeze. And there in the middle of the lake was the tin shack, no more than ten feet across, rusted, with a small covered terrace, sat on an island of sand and shrubs not much bigger.

We climb into the boat and as we untie it and push off, Harambe drops a hooked fish into the water, dragging it behind us while we row. Reaching the island, he tells us to grab the rope and tie the boat to the terrace post.

As we are tying a second knot, the stillness suddenly breaks and a crocodile lunges out of the water onto the sand, holding the hook and fish in its jaws. Harambe shouts to grab a rope and before we know what has happened, he pulls a large knife and sticks it in the belly of the beast, pulling it along its flank towards him. The ancient reptile goes wild and there is blood everywhere, some from the puncture wound, some from Harambe's arm. Both lay there panting, until the crocodile doesn't anymore and Harambe is laughing. We stand there in shock, then wrap Harambe's wounds. That evening, we eat fresh fish and crocodile meat on the fire. When we ask him if he knew, he says he didn't, but we don't believe him. Then he grins and says of course he did, what's why we came, that was the point.

HARRY

Harambe and I are like yin and yang, so different but also the same in so many ways. He is a gentle soul and a storyteller.

I teach him how to work with his hands, to make shoes or drill a well. He shows me how to tell the difference between momma clouds which look like udders and giant cumulus pillars and what the weather shall be. He tells me I have the spirit of a journeyman and a troubadour.

When he introduced me to Gabrielle, I fell in love instantly, but she only loved Harambe. We spent many times all three of us together and he would never know of how she adored him, though I suspect she always saw my unrequited love.

He introduced me to Herve, and we did not get on. We are too different, his temperament is volatile and I never know what is going to happen, though I can see why they are such friends. One day we almost come to blows, but Harambe asks us both to be together, in the charming way he always did.

Beside a fire one night, underneath the clear and starry sky, I tell him a story which he loves. I play my ukelele whilst I remember the true tale of a Chinese singer and spy who had an affair with a French politician and caused a riotous scandal. I try to remember more but it is enough for him.

We revel together in the grand improbability of life and the even greater possibility of more, which he says he sees always and everywhere, but eludes him when he tries to grasp or describe it. When we walk through woods, he speaks to the trees and touches his hand to their bark and buds. He says that trees have lives of great complexity like us, and that their roots extend far beyond their boundary. They know every step we take over the ground, speaking and listening with all that live by their side and in their branches. His reverence creates a sense of awe and oneness, and the peace is transcendent.

I once asked him, if you were to take away everything you had ever been told, what would you know. He considered this for a very long time, before he answered with the story of the lost man. He told how there was once a man who had lived on praise and pride and only wanted more, when he found all around him people who had only wanted less. And they looked upon the man with sympathy and benevolence, because those were the only ways they had known, shown by others who knew the way. And so they cast their kindness towards him with understanding and love. And his sadness turned to thanks and he became the found man.

THE MARKET TRADER

From the moment he arrives humming to himself, he picks up and inspects everything on the tables, fascinated and delighted by the small boxes and bird skulls and other curio I am selling.

He settles on a small brass heron, which he inspects thoroughly, as if looking for something. Then he offers me a deal, either the money in his left hand, or a small pouch in his right, which he says is much more interesting. I decline politely, intrigue doesn't put food on the table I tell him with a smile, and he grins back, putting the bird down and saying he will return later.

As he leaves, he bumps into another man and laughs, before wandering off into the throng.

Sometime later, I notice that the heron is gone. I look around for the man, who is nowhere to be seen, though I am sure he is still here. I am left with the feeling the heron has flown and I shall not see it nor the man again.

THE LAWYER

This man has the audacity of a politician and the ego of a priest, which compels me to listen to his request. He seeks my counsel in a private business deal, in which he says he doesn't want money, but something much rarer and infinitely more valuable. He explains the circumstances, which only creates further intrigue on my part, for he withholds as much as he tells. He pays me in cash and I prepare the paperwork.

When he returns the next day to sign the documents, he shakes my hand and offers his gratitude, and I never see him again.

A few weeks later, a small parcel arrives. Inside I find a small brass heron and with it, a note thanking me for my diligence and advice. He says he could not be more pleased and that the bird is a special gift which has flown a long way, an extra thank you for my valuable time.

THE DEALER

He unwraps the small pair of paintings that have been carefully secured in brown paper. He hasn't told me where he got them, but it becomes clear what they are as he lays them flat on the bench and we both admire them for a long time.

When they sell a month later for a king's ransom, I arrange for payment to be sent to the lawyer's account he has requested, minus my commission.

The day after, the lawyer sends me a box containing a small pouch in which I find a single opal, and a hand-written note telling me to hold on to it until further notice.

I never heard or saw Harambe or his lawyer again and after many years, I gave the opal to my daughter as a wedding gift.

CLEO

I meet Harambe by the door of the jazz club. His seven-colour hair reminds me of a fairy. As we walk and talk though city gardens and squares, I am smitten. Together, we are like children again, wandering in wonder, believing in magic, and talking of other worlds.

Later, when we are back at my apartment, I offer him some biscuits I had made the day before, but something changes in him and the way he refuses makes me think he is afraid I have poisoned them. When I ask if he is okay, he murmurs something, but I am not sure he is there, as if he had been suddenly removed from this world and transported a great distance away.

I never saw him again after that day, but think about him often, and lost loves that could have been.

HERVE

In the deserts of Utah and Texas we found nothing.
In Patagonia we found the brontosaurus, in Mumbai the opium dealers, and in Morocco the brothels.
In London and Paris we found waifs and strays and absinthe.
In the jungles of West Africa we found cannibals, in the snows of the Himalayas we found footprints, and in the fields of France we found mushrooms and symphonies.
And there, finally, beside the river, we found peace and in its waters the elixir of life.

PACHO II

We are sitting on a knife-edge between sense and reason and a madness derived from exploring the bowels of the mind and finding more than we bargained. We know we are not insane, but by reasonable standards we have opened our mind too much, we sometimes wonder, such that our brain might fall out.

The inferno at our feet is grabbing, lurching, kicking and biting to be fed. I let it linger close enough to dare, before it retreats to mellow and burn, the heat rippling down to embers and smoke.
I hold the mirror up for us both to see. It breaks into ten thousand pieces and now everything is sharp and raw and we cannot look away. If I am going to die, make it happen hard. It smarts but is painless. You can't kill me, I say, but you can try while you submit to my will.
He screams let's burn this whole goddamn place to the ground and build from the ashes a new beginning.
You and I are mad my friend, crazy as they come, immortal man-gods. Now let every heartbeat be

your first and last.

So we continue together on our journey where we tread carefully, eyes and mind wide open, for fear of falling into a cauldron so deep, we may never return.

HARAMBE I

My eyes are closed tight, and I am at the centre of a seemingly infinite space, the end of which I cannot see, illuminated with spherical prisms of every colour and extending in all directions from my centre. They hang like marbles in the air, some nearly touching, others leaving vast space in between.

I am no longer senses, male nor female, but sensations, vibrations of light, gravity and more. I am no longer time or space, I am everything everywhere.

And now I can see clearly the spheres together are a singular clock, each orb a moment of time in harmony, and I understand this perfect clock to be my life, and all other life, observed through a lens of vast dimension and proportion, in a way one cannot comprehend in a thousand lifetimes, laying at the end and the beginning of everything. Questions and answers spill together and I hear it speak.

Once there was infinite nothing, but to know itself it became all. And from the centre of nothing came everything. Now dwell in existence and acceptance, be an infinite vessel to receive what you need and give what you must. Listen to the invisible, for that is the voice of the universal and the key and door to your truth. Now breathe the essence in and exhale the spirit out, servant and master of effortless manifestation.

SANDRA

He didn't say much, he didn't need to. We met on a bench above the cliffs, watching the waves fold back and forth for a very long time.

We talked a little of mango trees and spinning wool, all the time staring from the breaking waves to the horizon.

He wore scars and recited poetry from memory, with a weathered face and a soft soul.

After a long while and a little rain, he mentioned something about a 'prison of our own making' but I couldn't quite hear. When I asked him to repeat it, he replied 'It's been really wonderful, thank you."

And then he disappeared, strolling down the steps to the beach where I watched as he drew circles in the sand until the tide washed them away and the sun went down behind the clouds.

ROYALE

We first met as young men when he helped my little brother in the street one day, after collapsing during one of his seizures.

Later over a game of cards and a box of cigars, when I caught Harambe cheating, I shot off the end of his thumb. He called me a psychopath and I agreed with him, but we were to be friends nonetheless, there is more to life and friendship than missing fingertips.

After he has left, I find he has stolen an opal from my office and it seems a fair trade. We remained friends for many years.

Some two years had passed since the last time I saw him, though we had spoken often. He had changed and looked much older than I remembered, as if life had finally caught up. He was quieter and had a melancholy about him which only further softened his voice and demeanour. We spoke about family, health and the usual, but it wasn't like before and I knew it might be the last time we met.

WHITE FEATHER

We are strangers sitting together on the promenade. He asks me my name and I tell him White Feather. He introduces himself as Harambe and admires my cowboy boots. I tell him they were a gift from a woman I once loved.

A few moments pass in comfortable silence, when a white feather falls from the sky landing beside us on the sandy kerb. As he holds it up at me in disbelief, I think to add it to my collection, when he takes off his hat and pushes it into a gap in the cloth. He tells me he will remember this moment for a very long time.

We share a smoke and he thanks me, then leaves on a bicycle to find breakfast. I see the white feather disappear into the distance and wave to the back of the mystery man.

JON THE BAPTIST

Every week he passes by my book stall outside the train station. He asks after my kids and we exchange genuine well-wishes and reassurance. He strokes my dog and I thank him for stopping by again.
He never buys a book, but always looks through and gives me a hug before he leaves, even though he is well-dressed and I am filthy and usually drunk.
He told me once that he spoke Pashtun and Swahili and kept a secret treasure chest under his bed, and that he left home at fifteen years old to hitchhike his way to Budapest.
I couldn't work out if he was telling the truth, or a storyteller of tall tales and imaginary worlds. But it never mattered, we just shared these brief moments for what they were.

THE DOCTOR

He didn't speak for a very long time after he arrived. When he finally did, he wanted to know if he had been in a dream. I asked him if he knew where he was and how he got here.

His daughter would visit regularly, tending his comforts, and he would occasionally look up with deep conversation in his eyes.

One day, he told me about the seven ancient wonders of the world and how the hanging gardens were a gift from a king to his wife who missed the hills of home, such was the love he had for her.

When eventually he left, we found a postcard and a small packet of seeds on his bedside table. On the card was a picture of an apple tree and on the back was written 'Dear Harambe, Once upon a time, there was a story, which didn't matter, didn't make sense, and wasn't true'. The nurses planted the seeds in the hospital gardens, and I kept the postcard which sits folded in my wallet to this day.

MIA

His head is tilted on the pillow and he stares out at the sky through the closed window. He tells me again what I have heard him say many times before, that we are all children of the infinite, borne of stars, mystery and beauty beyond our deepest imagination and dreams. He says life is a great dance of energy, earth, sky, animal and plant, and everything in between together in rhythm. We must each of us be a vessel of love, with strength and courage and kindness.

I kiss him on the forehead and shuffle to the end of the bed. His are eyes are closed and his breathing deep and slow. I close my eyes for a long time and listen. When I open them again, he has gone.

Tears of joy roll down my cheeks as I smile in wonder of this life complete, thankful for having known his love.

After a while, I pick up the miniature kaleidoscope from his pillow where it has fallen, and leave.

HARRY, CLARK AND MOONDOG

Harry, Clark and Moondog sat in the fading sunlight. I bet Jesus loved a beer, said Clark. I bet he liked to make beautiful love, said Moondog. Harry rocked in his chair not saying or doing anything.

A girl in a blue dress walked past and all three followed the hem and smiled. Younger years and all that.

Clark slammed the table and called the waiter. Beers and whiskey. Harry passed Clark a cigarette while Moondog rolled his own.

Music played faintly in the background, getting lost on the evening breeze, while candles flickered on the tables.

The drinks arrived, with Noah's compliments, and they charged their glasses to Harambe.

Harry closed his eyes, Moondog howled and Clark shot a gun in the air. They drank their whisky and sipped at their beers and then sat there for a while saying nothing.

HARAMBE II

The music is pounding in my head and chest. I am breathing hard, running up the concrete stairwell, three steps at a time, faster, higher and higher, breath louder and louder until I reach the top and burst through the door, into sky and eternity.

I stop and my breathing slows and slows until calm and steady. I stand still and quiet at the edge, before I leap from the roof and as a burst upon the ground, I explode into a hundred fragments of colour and light and flutter in the brightness of the day.

A thousand pieces of me move along the street, my energy in flow with life all around me, in sounds and sights and eyes and ears in bars and clubs and queues, on foot, on bike, everywhere I turn in rhythm.

We move along into the night, as new and different sights and sounds drift in and out, and the mood changes and now there is electricity in the air and something must happen.

PART 3
Notes from a Collection

An elderly gentleman was discovered with his manhood in a horse's mouth. The owner of the field on the outskirts of a small rural village assaulted the man with a stick, causing the horse to run off.

Police were called and arrested the 82 year old, who protested his innocence, saying he wasn't harming anybody.

He was charged with indecent exposure and is due before magistrates.

SANDRA.
Cliff bench. Waves. Mangos.
Wool spinning. Three kids
and abusive husband.

HOUSE PARTY GIRL.
Necklace and bracelets. Curly
hair. Delicious smell.
Collects quotes.

ZARATHUSTRA MAN.
Lion's mane. Rum. Middle
Finger. Wife. Shisha. Obelisk.

JON.
Books. Station. Dog. Four kids.
Joy and love. Barber.

SOME THINGS I
FOUND OR ACQUIRED

Giant African wasp (dead)
Green army poncho
Pink and green opal
Stone from war memorial
Brass heron
Sheep skull
Crocodile tooth
Porcupine needles
Striped tobacco pouch
Small pink toy (buried)
Oak marble gall
Chess pawn (white)
Peacock feather
Miniature ceramic bowl
Paradoxical Commandments
Tibetan Book of the Dead
Page from The Attic Nights
Cocktail bar menu
Roger's apple seeds

MANQUE
To fail to become what one could have been

HARAMBE
A Kenyan tradition meaning to all pull together

KINTSUKUROI
The Japanese art and philosophy of mending broken pottery with gold lacquer, to make it more beautiful than it was.

MICROMORT
A unit of risk measured in a one-in-a-million chance of death

SCOPOPHILIA
Pleasure from watching and looking at things and people

HARRY'S STORY

A Chinese opera singer was at the centre of an international spy scandal involving a love affair with a French politician. After persuading him that she was a woman, though appearing in public as a man, she collected secret documents and gave them to the Communist Party back in Beijing. This continued for nearly twenty years, including later being presented back in France as the politician's son. Both were later imprisoned, before receiving presidential pardons.

MARGOT'S POEM

If all that was is only time
And all I gave was never mine
If rich were poor, the poor are old
And thick of skin the softest souled
If pain and pleasure are equal in gain
And all ideas are parts of the same
If all you seek is all you find
And fear and joy are pure of mind
If gods don't care of life and death
And ebb and tide are right and left
If all of thought is all that's real
And all that is, is how you feel
If time to mend is time to part
Then time to end is time to start

PACHO'S BALLAD

I met myself at the crossroads
and dared myself to play
I rolled the dice and staked my soul
to see another day

I lost and he accepted
My soul for all of time
But gave me in return to keep
A tale to call all mine

It started at a crossroads
With game of dice and chance
A mirror and a madman
And a devil in a dance